For Chantelle and Sophie

Henry Holt and Company, LLC
Publishers since 1866
115 West 18th Street
New York, New York 10011

Henry Holt is a registered trademark of Henry Holt and Company, LLC

Text copyright © 1999 by Macmillan Publishers Limited
Illustrations copyright © 1999 by David Axtell
All rights reserved.
First published in the United States in 2000 by Henry Holt and Company, LLC.
Originally published in the United Kingdom in 1999 by Macmillan Children's Books,
a division of Macmillan Publishers Limited, London.

Library of Congress Cataloging-in-Publication Data
We're going on a lion hunt / illustrated by David Axtell.
Summary: Two girls set out bravely in search of a lion, going through
long grass, a swamp, and a cave before they find what they're looking for.
[1. Lions—Fiction.   2. Africa—Fiction.]   I. Axtell, David, ill.
PZ7.W4712 1999   [E]—DC21   98-47507

ISBN 0-8050-6159-2 / First American Edition   2000
Printed in Belgium
1   3   5   7   9   10   8   6   4   2

WE'RE GOING ON A
LION HUNT

David Axtell

Henry Holt and Company · New York

W e're going on a lion hunt.
We're going to catch a big one.
We're not scared.
Been there before.

We're going on a lion hunt.

We're going to catch a big one.

We're not scared.

Been there before.

Oh, no . . .

Long grass!

Can't go *over* it.

Can't go *under* it.

Can't go *around* it.

Have to go *through* it.

Swish, swash, swish, swash.

We're going on a lion hunt.

We're going to catch a big one.

We're not scared.

Been there before.

Oh, no . . .

A lake!

Can't go *over* it.

Can't go *under* it.

Can't go *around* it.

Have to go *through* it.

Splish, splash, splish, splash.

We're going on a lion hunt.

We're going to catch a big one.

We're not scared.

Been there before.

Oh, no . . .

A swamp!

Can't go *over* it.

Can't go *under* it.

Can't go *around* it.

Have to go *through* it.

Squish, squash, squish, squash.

We're going on a lion hunt.

We're going to catch a big one.

We're not scared.

Been there before.

Oh, no . . .

A Big Dark Cave!

Can't go *over* it.

Can't go *under* it.

Can't go *around* it.

Have to go *through* it.

In we go,
Tiptoe, tiptoe.

But **what's that?**

One shiny wet **nose!**

One big shaggy **mane!**

Four big furry **paws!**

It's a lion!

Back through the cave.
Back we go.

Tiptoe, tiptoe.

Back through the swamp.

Squish, squash, squish, squash.

Back through the lake.

Splish, splash, splish, splash.

Back through the long grass.

Swish, swash, swish, swash.

All the way home.

Slam the door—
CRASH!

We're all tired now.
Tired and sleepy.

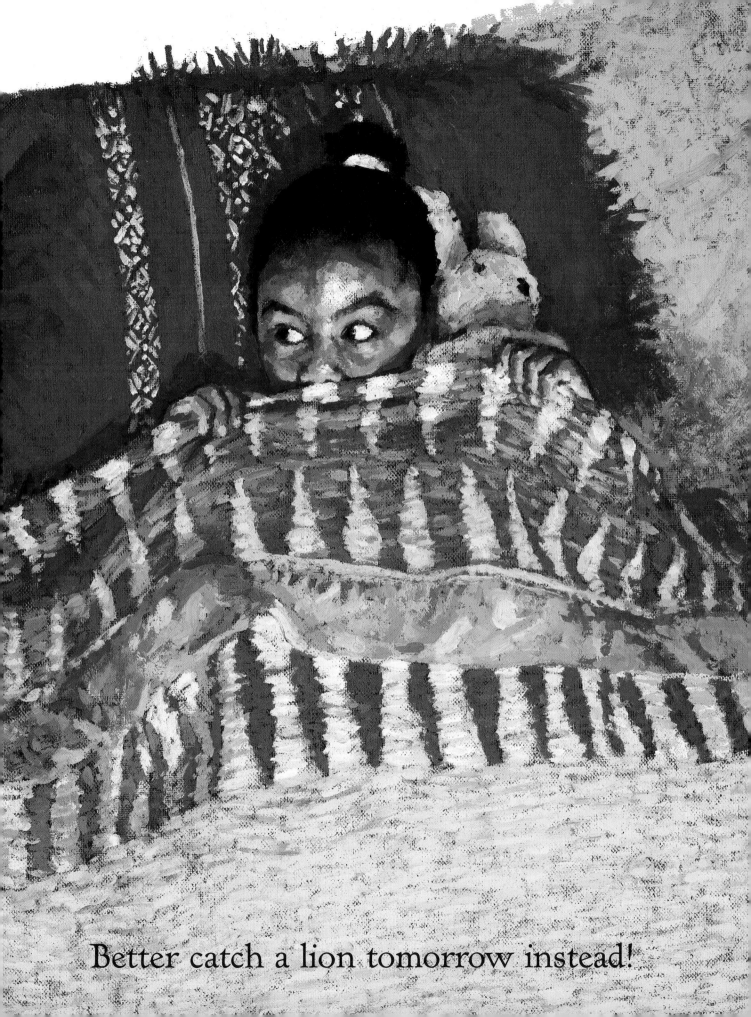

Better catch a lion tomorrow instead!

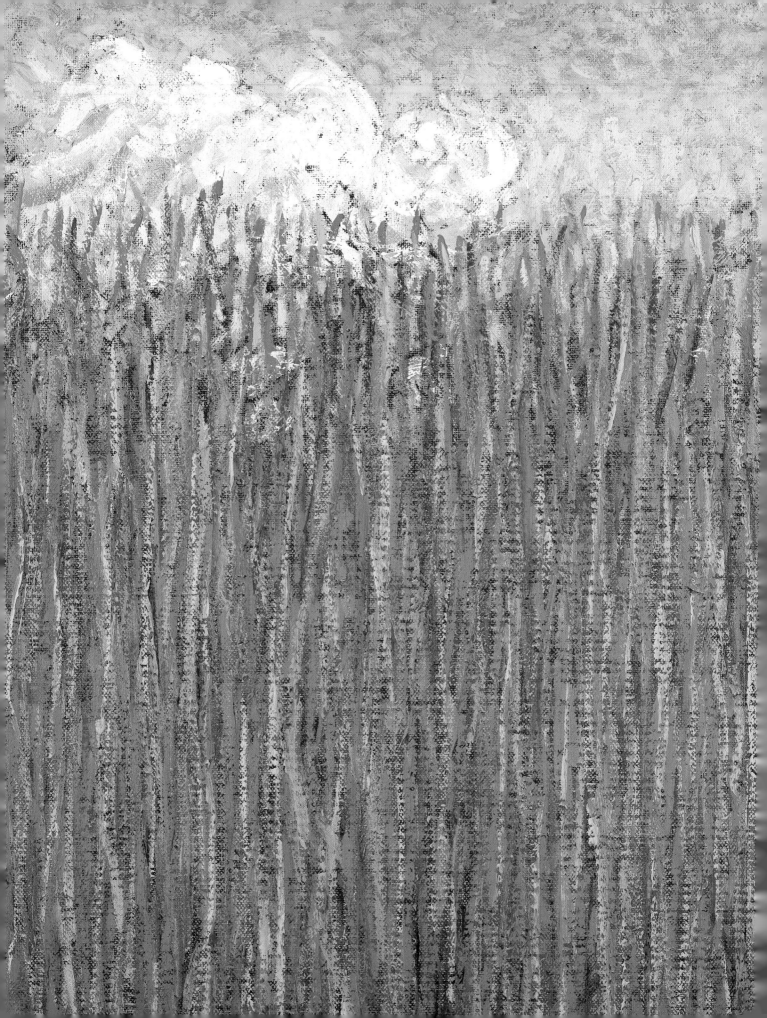